EPIPHANIES

MAYUKH MISHRA

To

Dr. Sujata Sahu

For listening to my silences even before they form a thought.

Contents

Contents

Contents

Acknowledgements

With immense gratitude, I dedicate *Epiphanies* to the many forces that have shaped its existence. To the unseen yet ever-present muse within my soul, thank you for weaving chaos into words and turning fleeting moments into timeless revelations.

To my family and friends, your unwavering support has been the lighthouse guiding me through the creative storm. Your belief in my words gave me the courage to pour my heart onto these pages.

To the countless readers, dreamers, and seekers who inspired this work—know that your experiences and emotions resonate within these words. This book would not exist without the universal tapestry of human connection.

To the infinite wisdom of life itself, with its unpredictable rhythms and profound lessons, thank you for reminding me that beauty often emerges from the unexpected.

Finally, to *you*, dear reader, thank you for opening this book and embarking on this journey with me. May these epiphanies spark a few of your own.

1

Aum Shiv Shambhu

He is the embodiment of the most profound, pristine, and exquisite contours of my heart—a black, all-encompassing presence, both transcendent and intimate. Chaotic yet sublime, distracted yet focused, nuanced yet fervent. On the quietest days, I can hear him breathing, feel the soft rhythm of his existence, and sense his silent embrace, as inevitable and all-encompassing as gravity drawing atoms into its fold—gentle at first, then utterly consuming.

I love him with the unguarded abandon of a strand of hair cast adrift on a sunlit shore, with the lingering warmth of an embrace long remembered, with the purity of silence birthing thought, and the audacious harmony of colours colliding in fearless exploration. His silence carries the resonance of divinity—a sacred hymn that reverberates with the comfort of voluntary inclusion, the seamless merging of souls, and the transformative essence of a love that transcends the tangible.

2

Tara

She arrived not with footsteps but with the whisper of leaves, her shadow woven from twilight, her voice a hymn of forgotten stars. Her eyes, deep as the cosmos, held galaxies of longing, and her touch lingered like dew, ephemeral yet eternal. She speaks in riddles of the wind and the secrets of rivers that carve their way into stone. When she laughs, time stumbles; when she weeps, the earth trembles, birthing flowers in the most desolate corners.

I saw her on the edge of sleep, where dreams bleed into the waking world. Her presence wraps around me like moonlight on restless seas, quiet yet all-consuming. Her dance on my skin is like the first rain kissing parched earth, like the flicker of fireflies in a dense forest, like ink spilling into water, creating constellations of evading memories. She is magic made flesh, reality tinged with the impossible—a moment stretched into eternity, a love that reshapes the laws of the universe with every breath falling short a moment before life.

3

Wet Meadows

We ran, like a lost train without direction, our bare feet grazing the earth, brown in opulence like our skins after the primal shower. The meadow, damp with morning dew, embraced her with a gentle coolness, while the scent of earth and wildflowers filled the air of my lungs. There was no hurry in her steps, only the soft, rhythmic pulse of her heartbeat keeping pace with the wind that danced through my now lost signs. Each footfall was a silent declaration of radical freedom, of unspoken desires and dreams. The grass, heavy with dew, brushed against her skin like an intimate caress, leaving fleeting traces that lingered only for a moment, yet were etched in my soul forever. She was lost in the simplicity of the moment, her heart swelling with a love as wild and untamed as the first hunt of a forsaken beast.

The world around us seemed to fade into the background, and there was only the rush of her breath, the laughter of the wind, and the sweet melody of the earth beneath our skin. She ran as if she could outrun time, as if each step carried her closer to a place where only love and freedom existed far way from the rules of the world. In that moment, she was more than just a woman running on wet grass—she was the embodiment of every unspoken word, every quiet yearning, every hidden dream. Her feet were the language of her heart, telling stories in the language of the earth, of a love so pure, it could only be felt beneath the vast expanse of my heart that watched over her; shy, silent and eternal.

4

Cactus

In the heart of life's summer, when the earth feels like it's burning underfoot and the sky seems to press down with its weight, the cactus stands. Its body is a fortress—thick skin and sharp spines—an armour forged by the harshest of conditions. Each thorn a façade protruding out of struggles it has endured, each prick a response of the pain we often feel, buried deep within. But then, against all odds, a flower begins to bloom. At first, it opens timidly, as though testing the air, unsure if it can survive the darkness that surrounds it.

The sun beats down mercilessly, the desert winds cut sharp as blades, and yet this fragile blossom dares to stretch its petals toward the sky. Slowly, it unfurls, each delicate curve of its white petals a soft, defiant whisper in the face of everything that wants to crush it. This flower, it doesn't resist the summer; it surrenders to it, accepting its presence with quiet strength. And in doing so, it becomes something extraordinary. In the midst of a world that would rather break you, it blooms—beautiful, vulnerable, and full of life.

5

Dive

When I speak, a realm unfurls within—an expanse woven from the threads of celestial eclipses. Words clash, like opposing forces in an unseen war, sentences locking in silent combat, each seeking dominion. My tongue sways to an elusive cadence, a melody of its own design, while my breath, like an ancient healer, gently tends to the discord, drawing them into delicate consonance.

What is this breath, that moves through the chaos, whispering the secrets of life and death? Sometimes lost in the shadows of forgetfulness, yet always returning, it cradles within it the timeless hymns of the divine, songs unspoken yet eternally resonating. It is both the tempest and the stillness, the unseen pulse that knits together the ruptured fragments of existence.

6

Descent into Unseen

The siren wails, a banshee's cry that shatters the stillness of my thoughts. It rings, relentless and cruel, as the mask I once wore—my fragile guise of sanity—cracks and falls away. Unmasked, raw with trembling, I stumble upon my own insignificance, yet I race with no direction, no purpose. The stairs before me rise, jagged and unforgiving, like the broken faces of those I have failed. Each ascent is a new torment, each rung a whisper of my inadequacy. I clutch at the air, grasping for something solid, anything to anchor me in the free-fall of my mind. Somehow, my feet find the ground—drenched in sweat and shaking, trembling with potent rage, and I stand, though unsteady as a drowning man grasping for a fleeting breath. My lungs, once calm, now scream for air, gasping for something I cannot reach. The breath that soothed me, now strangled by the weight of fear, stutters in and out like a dying flame.

An opaque dread, thick as sawdust, wraps itself around my chest, suffocating me with its cold embrace. The world around me warps, a suffocating blur as the shadows close in. The light, once a guide, now flickers weakly, swallowed involuntarily by an impending darkness that feels alive, hungry, waiting. I close my eyes, not because I am tired, but because I want to escape spiritedness. The sight of it all—this terrifying vastness of nothingness—becomes too much to bear. The light is lost, swallowed whole, its death marked by the birth of something darker, something endless. And I, a wretched thing caught in the undertow of my own mind, feel myself drifting farther from reality, sinking into the abyss where no sound, no breath, no hope can follow.

7
Museum of Innocence

I am a museum of innocence, a curator of fleeting moments, and yet, I am also the lost visitor wandering through its halls. My footsteps echo in the silence, unsure of where to pause—caught between the delicate, slender fingers writing onto itself like the last breath of a forgotten dream, and the ocean of her eyes, vast and unknowable, where a moon hangs suspended above a limping rabbit, its gait as uneven as the path I cannot find. They—those quiet, trembling parts of her—smile when they sense my gaze, as if the world itself bends to the unspoken touch of a glance. In that smile, a flower unfurls, its petals trembling as though unsure if it should bloom in the light of such a transient moment. The visitor within me, lost in the swirl of this transmorphism, weeps with a joy too heavy for words—a gravitational joy that pulls me deeper into her, into us, into something impossible to hold.

The fluttering of my fingers, like leaves caught in a windless moment, crave to pluck those flowers in the autumn of her presence, to capture them before they fall into the transient spring of time. Yet, I know I cannot. The flowers will bloom and wither, just as we will. But for now,

I remain—a visitor, a wanderer in this museum of innocence, where the beauty of it all exists only in the yearning, the ache, the ungraspable fragility of what could be.

8
Butterflies

Butterflies, born of sweltering sand, dissolve into the heat before they can take flight, vanishing only to return as confetti—delicate sparks of light, flickering and merging in multitudes of silent epiphanies. They shimmer in the air, fleeting as thoughts that cross the mind and dissipate before they can be named. Sunshine at midnight, a defiant anomaly, wears its heart with unguarded grace, splashing the darkness with an innocence only the stars might envy. It spills warmth as it wraps itself around the cold, making the night tremble with its vulnerability. A serpent, not of malice but of affectionate attention, coils languidly around a finger—its touch both gentle and possessive.

In this space, a name exists, not as mere sound, but as a glowing sigil within the circle of another universe—a name that pulses with an energy beyond comprehension, as though it is not of this world but from one where time and space bow to its essence. A puff of breath, once full of intent, disintegrates in wanton abandon, unravelling into the ether with the same quiet defiance that defines the fragile beauty of the moment. It is gone before it is fully realized, and yet, in its absence, a profound truth remains—one that lives in the spaces between the words, between the breaths, between the seconds that fall like stars into the unknown.

9
Web of Fate

In the noises of the stolen shadows, a spider waits, its eight limbs poised in dramatic stillness, each movement calculated, each pause deliberate. The web, an intricately spun with precision, glistens in the faintest sliver of light, a shimmering snare of love and care. It is not merely a trap—it is a story, a poem composed in the language of silk and waiting venom. A flutter breaks the stillness—a tremor in the air. The prey arrives, unaware of the delicate threads stretching just beyond its reach of snarling innocence. Its tiny body brushes against the web, and in that instant, time bends. The spider's legs move with the fluid grace of a predator's dance, each step carrying the weight of inevitability. The web trembles as the prey, caught in the soft, invisible threads, struggles in a frantic, futile attempt to break free.

But there is no escape. The more it writhes, the more it sinks deeper into the web, drawn into the spider's inviting embrace. The predator moves with purpose now, its fangs gleaming in the dim light, as it wraps its prize in silk—a final, tender act of possession, of fate sealed in the most delicate of threads. The spider's gaze, cold and unwavering, lingers on the prey—no hatred, no malice, only the acknowledgment of what must be.

10
Dance of Silence

The musician and the dancer are like lovebirds, bound by an unspoken understanding, their spirits intertwined in an intimate harmony. In the stillness of their connection, they do not need words. Their eyes meet and silently cast a spell, a gaze that speaks more than any phrase ever could. Each understands the other's movements and breath, as if their hearts beat in the same rhythm. There is an elegance in this unspoken language, a dance of silence where every glance, every gesture, is a verse in their mutual song.

They know when to bend, when to surrender, and when to hold steady. In the ebb and flow of their performance, they reach a point where the art and the artist become indistinguishable. The boundaries blur, and what remains is a purity of expression, a complete renunciation to the moment. If one falters, if a beat is missed, they forgive without hesitation—because in their dance, there is no judgment. There is only understanding and the quiet knowledge that the heart contains deeper emotional secrets, treasures that they can share in that very instant.

Their love burns solely for itself, casting a soft, private light. It does not seek an audience, nor does it require validation. It burns quietly, steadily, its glow absorbed by the essence of the fire itself. And when the music ends, when the dance stops, what remains is not the flame, but its warmth—the lingering impression of something pure, something timeless, that only the musician and dancer will ever truly understand.

11

Maa

Nursing a child is a ritual steeped in ancient grace, a silent covenant between the giver and the receiver, where the body becomes both temple and sanctuary. In this sacred act, time slips into suspension, the world's clamour fading into a hushed reverence. The infant, its mouth soft and searching, seeks the breast not just for sustenance, but for a deeper communion—its hunger a prayer, its cries a hymn, while the mother's breast, a fountain of life, offers not just milk but the essence of being itself.

The mother's body, a fertile garden, feeds the child not merely with nourishment but with the sustenance of her soul. Each drop of milk carries with it the stories of generations—of the bloodlines, the histories, the eternal threads of lineage passed down through time. In this moment, the child is cradled not only in her arms but in the warm cradle of the universe itself, held in the embrace of an ancient, unbroken lineage.

As the child drinks, it is as though the very fabric of life is being rewoven, as if the heart of the mother is being shared, little by little, with her child, an offering of self that knows no end. There is a beauty in the simplicity of the gesture, an otherworldly grace in the quiet exchange, where the act of feeding is a gift of life passed from one soul to another.

12

Paradox

It is a cycle, a salt-and-pepper paradise where the sands meet the sea in a ceaseless waltz. A monotonous conundrum of waves, unfaltering in their rhythm, kiss the shores with an almost invisible persistence. The ocean, ever-stretching, cloaks its brutality beneath the guise of beauty, luring the weary and the hopeful alike. Ask the fishermen who have lost sons to the cruel tides, their eyes hollow with the weight of a promise the sea never kept. Ask the little girl, tears streaking down her face, whose favourite toy was swallowed whole by the indifferent waves. Ask the young boys, their ankles scraped and raw, the remnants of their games carved into the sand as the ocean erases them.

The heart of the ocean is vast and devouring, a silent predator wrapped in the façade of a beauty that knows no bounds. Its pulse is the rhythm of loss, its depth the secret of countless lives swallowed in its eternal hunger. And what remains? A mirage. A fleeting illusion that flickers and fades with the ebb and flow, leaving behind only the scent of salt on the air, and the memory of a beauty that hides its true face behind waves that never cease.

13

I Seek

I do not seek a chiselled physique adorned with cosmetic cuts, nor a camera-loving Adonis basking in fleeting adulation. I do not long for a self-adoring Narcissus, forever entranced by his own reflection, chasing a beauty that evades him like a mirage. They sprint through anxious lanes, loathing their own splendour because it is never quite enough. They soar toward their suns, only to weep over melted wings and singed dreams.

I seek the beauty of a spoiled puff, laughter spilling out between mouthfuls of ice cream, sticky hands and carefree grins. I seek imperfections wearing their humility like a crown, confident in their quiet authenticity. I long for flushed faces, aglow not with vanity but with the joy of shared stories and unguarded moments. I yearn for the kind of smile that lingers even as exhaustion sets in, and the kind of sleep that comes unbidden on lazy afternoons, wrapped in the warmth of home and unpretentious peace.

This is the beauty I seek—not carved from marble, but sculpted by the hands of life itself, tender and raw, imperfect yet profoundly whole.

14

Healing

Healing is not a straight road but a labyrinth, winding and uneven, where each step forward feels as though it carries the weight of a thousand yesterdays. It is the art of rebuilding with shards, a mosaic crafted from fragments of what was once whole.

At first, it is raw—a wound that demands attention, aching with every breath, throbbing with the memory of what broke you. Time doesn't rush in with grand solutions but offers small mercies: a quiet morning, a kind word, a fleeting moment of peace. Healing creeps in unnoticed, like ivy slowly reclaiming abandoned walls.

It is a rhythm—a hesitant waltz of pain and recovery. There are days when the scars itch, demanding to be reopened, and nights when silence screams louder than any wound. Yet, amidst the chaos, there is a subtle shift: the wound starts to close, not with perfection but with resilience.

Healing is a dialogue, an intimate conversation with oneself. It asks you to forgive, to grieve, to embrace vulnerability without shame. It teaches you to sit with the shadows, to honour the parts of yourself that were once silenced.

And then, one day, it happens—a lightness where there was once only weight. A smile that doesn't feel forced, a laugh that escapes without guilt. Healing is not a return to what was but an arrival at something new, something softer, something stronger. It is the gentle understanding that you are both the wound and the salve, the storm and the calm after.

Healing is not forgetting; it is transforming. It is the alchemy of pain into wisdom, brokenness into beauty, and survival into grace.

15

Forgiveness

Forgiveness is not a gift you give to others; it is a release you grant yourself. It is the quiet untangling of chains that bind you to a hurt long past, a liberation that whispers of peace in the chambers of a weary heart. At first, it feels impossible—a concession too great, a betrayal of your pain. The wound still throbs, and the memory of the wrong clings to you like a shadow. But forgiveness does not demand forgetfulness. It does not erase the ache or condone the act. Instead, it allows you to reclaim the space that resentment has stolen.

Forgiveness is a choice, deliberate and slow, like peeling away layers of grief. It is looking at the scar and saying, *you do not own me anymore.* It is a river flowing through a parched landscape, softening the hardened earth with each gentle touch. To forgive is to recognize the humanity in others and in yourself. It acknowledges frailty, imperfection, and the inevitability of missteps. It doesn't excuse the pain inflicted but refuses to let it define your future.

Forgiveness is not weakness. It is courage wrapped in tenderness. It is the strength to put down the burden of bitterness and walk forward, lighter, freer. It is the softening of the soul, the quiet dismantling of walls built to protect but which only imprisoned.

In the end, forgiveness is a kind of transformation, turning the poison of anger into the gold of understanding. It is not for the person who wronged you but for the person you are becoming—a person who chooses peace over pride, freedom over fury, and love over lingering sorrow.

16

Losing is Winning

Losing love feels like a theft—a sudden emptiness where fullness once lived, a silence where laughter echoed. It leaves you untethered, grasping at memories that dissolve like mist in the morning sun. At first, the void is unbearable, a wound too deep to touch, bleeding questions you can't yet answer. But in the quiet aftermath, something stirs. You sit with the emptiness, not to fill it, but to understand it. You trace the contours of your heart, now raw but still beating, and you realize: love is not gone, only misplaced.

Finding love within oneself is not a journey outward but inward, an exploration of the landscapes you forgot to visit when someone else held the map. It is rediscovering the small joys—the way your laughter sounds in an empty room, the comfort of your own company, the quiet magic of watching the world unfold without needing anyone to witness it with you. It is a reclamation, a remembering. You are reminded that your worth does not hinge on another's gaze, that your beauty exists even when unseen. You start to fall in love with your own resilience, with the way you rise despite the weight of sorrow, with the way you carry tenderness even after heartbreak.

And in time, the emptiness becomes a space for growth, a garden where new dreams take root. The love you sought outside now blooms within, radiant and unyielding. You become your own sanctuary, your own solace. Lost love teaches you that no one else completes you—they simply complement the love you already possess. And when you find it within, you realize you were never truly lost, only waiting to come home to yourself.

17

Adulting

Adulting arrives not with fanfare but in the quiet, unnoticed moments. It is the weight of unsaid responsibilities, the endless lists written in invisible ink, and the realization that no one is coming to save you—not from the deadlines, not from the broken faucet, not from yourself.

It is mornings that taste of burnt toast and coffee gone cold because you spent too long staring at bills and calendars. It is nights heavy with thoughts of choices made and paths untaken, of dreams traded for stability. Adulting is the art of balancing—balancing hope with reality, ambition with exhaustion, and the heart with the mind. It is learning to be your own parent, soothing the child within who still cries for simplicity. It's cooking meals for one, mending socks, calling the plumber, and finally understanding why your parents sighed at the end of the day. It is remembering birthdays without reminders and forgetting your own in the chaos of everything else.

But adulting is not just hardship. It is also the quiet pride in figuring things out. It is the small victories of folding laundry, of a well-seasoned meal, of saving just enough for a weekend escape. It is the understanding that perfection is a myth and that showing up is half the battle won. It is knowing that it's okay to break sometimes and to rebuild with trembling hands. It's finding joy in little things—a sunset caught on the way home, the smell of rain on a hard day, or the rare bliss of a day with no alarms.

Adulting is not about having it all figured out; it's about learning to carry the questions gracefully. It is the messy, beautiful journey of becoming—falling, rising, and making peace with the in-between. It is discovering that you are stronger than you thought and gentler than you believed, and that both are enough.

18

Old Love

Old love is a quiet flame, steady and enduring, burning with a warmth that doesn't seek to dazzle but to comfort. It is not the rush of first glances or the dizzying whirlwind of infatuation. Instead, it is the slow, deliberate weaving of two lives, a tapestry rich with shared moments, frayed edges, and patches stitched with care. Old love speaks in the language of familiarity. It is the knowing glance across a crowded room, the unspoken understanding that a sigh carries more than words ever could. It's the ease of shared silences, the kind that feels like a conversation rather than an absence.

Time weathers old love, softens its sharp edges, and polishes its core. The once fervent declarations are replaced by quiet acts of devotion—a hand reaching out in the dark, a favourite meal cooked without asking, the patient retelling of a story already heard a hundred times. But old love is not without its storms. It bears the marks of trials overcome, the echoes of arguments softened by forgiveness, and the scars that tell of wounds healed but not forgotten. It grows not because it is untested but because it endures, finding strength in vulnerability and grace in persistence.

Old love doesn't seek perfection; it embraces flaws. It is the recognition of each other's humanity—the quirks that once annoyed become the things you'd miss most; the imperfections are transformed into unique fingerprints on your shared life. It is a love that understands time's passage, that accepts the changes etched into faces and souls. It is the hand still held in old age, the voice that still calls you home, the steadfast presence that remains even when the world shifts beneath your feet. Old love is not a relic of the past but a testament to the present, a gentle reminder that the deepest connections are not fleeting—they are built, cherished, and nurtured over time. It is a sanctuary, a refuge, a legacy of two lives intertwined, growing stronger as they weather the years together.

19

Living Water

Living water is a paradox, a force that flows yet remains whole, soft yet unyielding, a quiet revolution shaping everything it touches. It does not shout its presence, yet its whispers carve mountains, wear down stone, and breathe life into the barren. In its clarity, there is a reflection—a mirror of what it holds and what it has seen. It moves with purpose, weaving through valleys and cradling life in its current. Each ripple is a story, each wave a reminder of resilience. It does not resist the obstacles it encounters; instead, it dances around them, finding a path where none existed before.

Yet, in its stillness, it holds a different kind of power. The surface, calm and unbroken, masks a world teeming beneath—an unseen depth where life pulses, unseen but present. In its silence, it becomes a sanctuary, a place where the weary find rest and the restless find clarity. Living water does not demand attention; it earns it. It nurtures without expectation, transforms without hesitation, and reminds us, in its quiet, persistent flow, that life is not a race to the end but a journey to be embraced, moment by moment, drop by drop.

20

Pregnant Sleep

Pregnant sleep is a world unto itself—a fragile equilibrium between exhaustion and creation. It is not mere rest but a quiet communion, a profound pause where two lives exist as one. The body, heavy with purpose, sinks deeply into the rhythm of the earth, each breath a tide that carries both the mother and the unborn into a shared dreamscape. It is a sleep interrupted, not by noise or unrest, but by the whispers of a life forming within—a gentle kick, a flutter, a reminder of the miracle unfolding in silence.

This sleep carries the weight of anticipation. It is filled with the echoes of the future—a soft lullaby hummed in the heart, a cradle rocking in the mind. Every dream feels deeper, every rest heavier, as though the body knows it is building a universe from within, cell by cell, heartbeat by heartbeat. And yet, in this sleep, there is also surrender. A letting go to the unknown, to the mystery of life itself. It is the kind of sleep that transforms, not with loud revelations, but with quiet resilience—a preparation for a love so profound it reshapes everything it touches.

21

Favourite Colour

Whiteness is a sanctuary—a canvas where silence speaks and simplicity thrives. It is not empty but full, holding the weight of all that is pure and unspoken. I wear white as if it were the sky draped around me—a saree flowing like quiet rivers under the moonlight. Each fold carries the essence of grace, each thread a testament to the softness i choose to carry. It is a colour that does not demand attention but invites it, gently, with the touch of timeless elegance.

The white roses in my hands are not mere flowers but offerings of my soul. Their petals, soft and unblemished, breathe the language of love and resilience. They bloom, even in the harshest moments, whispering truths that words cannot reach. My heart, too, is white—not for its innocence but for its clarity. It beats with the quiet strength of a flame, unyielding yet calm. In its chambers lies the balance of passion and peace, the ability to hold joy and sorrow in equal measure.

And then there is my hair, streaked with silver like threads of dawn breaking through the night. Each strand speaks of time, of transformation, of becoming. It is a map of experiences—each moment woven into the tapestry of who I am. Whiteness is not the absence of colour; it is the culmination of all shades. It holds life's paradoxes—fragility and power, emptiness and abundance, stillness and movement. It is a state of being, a metamorphosis in itself, where i find my becoming, over and over again.

22
House of Memories

The house breathes in the silence, exhaling dust and the scent of yesterday. Its wooden ribs creak under the weight of time, the walls still carrying the laughter of a child who once chased shadows through its corridors. The doorframe bears the inked whispers of growing years, a quiet invocation to hands that once measured love in inches. In the kitchen, the ghosts of old spices cling to the air, the echo of a mother's voice still simmering in the space between empty chairs. Outside, the swing sways with no one to claim it, the garden kneeling beneath the memory of small feet that once ran through its wild embrace. The house does not forget, even when the world does. It holds the stories we leave behind, waiting for us to return and read them again.

But time is an unkind keeper. It replaces warmth with silence, laughter with dust, presence with shadows. The wallpaper peels in places where hands once rested, the floorboards groan under the weight of ghosts that refuse to leave. I stand at the threshold, hesitant, knowing that some doors, once opened, cannot be closed again. The past does not greet me as it once did. It lingers at the edges, waiting for me to acknowledge its presence. I step inside, and for a moment, I am a child again, small and bright-eyed, unaware of the distance time would carve between us. The house exhales, and in its breath, I find the pieces of myself I thought I had lost.

23

Cartographer's Heart

He traced the map of me in slow, deliberate lines, his fingers mapping the ridges of my spine like uncharted land. Every breath between us was a new discovery, a whispered promise of constellations still unnamed. But love does not always linger where it is born. Some hands are made for holding, others for letting go. And so, he packed his compass and set sail beyond my horizon, leaving behind only the imprint of a touch that once knew me like home.

I search for him in the spaces he has left behind, in the air between my ribs, in the silence where his voice used to rest. I retrace our footsteps, hoping to find the path back to what we were, but the trail has faded, swallowed by time's steady tide. Love is a landscape that changes when you are not looking. It shifts beneath your feet, turns familiar places into foreign lands. I wonder if he still remembers the way back or if the map of me has become an unreadable blur. Some cartographers do not return to their maps, and some love stories are not meant to be found again.

24
Ritual of Rain

It begins in the hush before the first drop falls, in the stillness where the earth holds its breath. Then comes the rain, a slow unraveling, a symphony of liquid grace. The streets darken, the trees shudder with relief, and I step into the downpour as if it were a baptism, a cleansing of all that lingers beneath my skin. My hair clings to my face, my clothes to my body, but I am not drowning—I am being rewritten. The past dissolves into the pavement, the weight of old words slipping down the curve of my spine.

By the time the storm passes, I am lighter, washed clean of all that once felt permanent. But healing is not immediate, nor is it linear. The rain does not wash away everything—it leaves behind the parts of me that refuse to be undone. Some wounds heal in the open air, others fester beneath the surface, waiting for another storm to break them free. I listen to the rhythm of the droplets against the earth, each one a quiet reassurance that nothing is ever truly lost, only transformed. And as the clouds begin to part, I lift my face to the sky, letting the last remnants of sorrow trickle away.

25

Weight of an Unsent Letter

It sits in the drawer, folded into silence, a paper skeleton of words that never found their way to him. The ink has dried, but my hands still remember the shape of the confessions they once held. I tell myself that some things are better left unsaid, that the past should remain untouched. But on quiet nights, I hear the whisper of that letter calling to me, longing to be freed from its paper prison.

I imagine him reading it, his fingers tracing the edges of my truth, his lips shaping my name in a language we never spoke aloud. I wonder if he would have understood, if he would have looked at the words and seen the depth of what I never said. Perhaps he would have smiled, or perhaps he would have folded it away as if it were nothing more than another forgotten moment. The letter stays where it is, pressed between pages that will never be turned. Some stories do not need endings; they only need to exist, suspended in the delicate space between regret and possibility.

26

The Art of Vanishing

I have perfected the act of disappearing. Not in grand, dramatic exits, but in the quiet slipping away—leaving rooms before I am noticed, retreating into corners where shadows make homes out of people like me. I fold myself into silence, into the spaces between conversations, into the safety of being unseen.

But some days, I wonder if I have vanished too well, if I have erased myself so thoroughly that even I can no longer find my own reflection. Perhaps one day, I will unfold again, step into the light and let my edges become sharp enough to be recognized. But for now, I remain a whisper in a world too loud to hear me.

27

Museum of Forgotten Things

There is a museum where lost things are kept—the names we can no longer remember, the dreams we abandoned in the rush of living, the laughter that once shook our bones but now lies buried beneath the dust of time. The air hums with the quiet ache of nostalgia, the sound of seconds slipping through careless fingers. I walk its halls, running my hands over glass cases filled with echoes of who I used to be. In the corner, a single chair waits, as if expecting someone who will never return. I sit, close my eyes, and listen to the stories trapped in the walls, knowing that one day, I too will become part of the collection.

28

Silence

Silence is not empty. It is heavy, thick with the weight of everything we do not say. It sits between us like an uninvited guest, filling the spaces where words should be. I want to break it, to spill the truth onto the table between us, to let my voice crash against yours like waves against stone. But fear keeps my mouth closed, my tongue a prisoner behind the bars of my teeth. And so, we sit, two bodies drowning in the same quiet ocean, neither willing to reach for the other.

29

Hands

Before words, there were hands. Fingers that traced love into skin, palms that held lifetimes in their warmth. I have known hands that spoke in soft grazes and hands that trembled under the weight of unshed sorrow. Some hands fit so perfectly into mine that they felt like home. Others let go before I was ready, leaving behind only the ghost of their touch. I have learned that love is not always spoken—it is felt in the spaces where hands meet and in the emptiness when they no longer do.

30
Shape of a Scar

Scars are not merely marks on skin; they are stories etched into flesh, proof of battles fought and survived. My body is a map of past wounds, each scar a chapter, each line a testament to the way I have learned to heal. There was a time I wished them away, traced my fingers over them with shame. But now, I run my hands along their ridges with reverence, knowing they are not signs of weakness, but proof that I endured. I am a collection of healed fractures, a mosaic of survival, a body that has learned how to mend itself even after breaking.

31
Echoes of Forgotten Laughter

Laughter once resided here—unrestrained, spilling like liquid gold into forgotten spaces. Now, silence wraps around the walls, thick and unmoving. It does not grieve, nor does it celebrate. It merely lingers, vast and unyielding.

Ghosts of laughter drift through the air, caught in the rustle of curtains or the dance of dust motes in afternoon light. I listen, not with ears but with the marrow of my bones, waiting for its return. Perhaps, one day, it will break free—hesitant at first, like a hesitant tide reclaiming the shore. And when it does, it will not be the same, but it will be enough.

32
The Way I Speak

The way I speak is not an absence but a presence—a slow pulse beating beneath the skin of the world. It speaks in the weight of unshed tears, in the space between unsaid words, in the hush before dawn's arrival. It does not demand; it simply exists, unshaken, unspoken.

I have found refuge in its depths, where the world folds into itself. I holds truths words cannot bear, confessions caught in the moment before lips part. It carries longing, regret, and love suspended in quiet reverence. The way I speak is a double-edged thing—it can heal as much as it haunts, a paradox wrapped in shadow and light.

33

A House with No Address

Somewhere, beyond the reach of maps, there is a house suspended between past and present—a place neither lost nor found. It exists within the breath of nostalgia, its walls woven from longing and remembrance.

Windows frame a sky forever shifting, and floorboards murmur secrets beneath invisible footsteps. Here, time is an unreliable narrator, stretching moments into infinity, folding memories into the soft hush of dusk. The scent of monsoon-damp pages lingers in forgotten corners, and a mother's lullaby hums through the quiet air.

But homes, like memories, fade. Dust settles where laughter once bloomed, and silence fills the void where voices used to be. And yet, in dreams, I return—reaching for a doorknob smoothed by familiar hands, tracing the echoes of a place that exists only in the tender ache of recollection. For a moment, it is real again, until morning unravels the illusion, leaving only the whisper of something cherished yet untouchable.

34
Unfinished Poem

There is a poem I never wrote, a line that lingers just beyond my reach. It drifts in the quiet corners of my mind, unfinished yet complete in its longing. I can hear its rhythm in the hush of midnight, feel its pulse in the spaces between heartbeats. But when I try to give it form, it dissolves like mist, slipping through my grasp.

Perhaps some words are not meant to be caged in ink. Perhaps they exist only in the silent understanding of things left unsaid. I carry the poem within me, in the way my hands ache to write it, in the way my soul knows its cadence without ever speaking it aloud. It is not a loss but a presence, an unspoken verse that lives in the spaces between breath and silence.

35

The Weight of an Empty Chair

An empty chair is never truly vacant—it holds the shape of absence, the echo of someone who once filled its space. It is a silent witness to conversations unfinished, laughter that once rang through the air, moments that remain suspended in time.

I pass by it each day, resisting the urge to fill the void it has become. It belongs to the past now, a relic of something once whole. Yet, in its stillness, it speaks. It whispers of hands that once gripped its arms, of weary sighs that settled into its fabric, of presence turned into memory.

Perhaps one day, someone else will sit there, unaware of the weight they inherit. Or perhaps it will remain as it is—a monument to what was, a quiet keeper of stories no longer told aloud.

36

When Rain Meets the Ocean

There is a moment, fleeting yet eternal, when raindrops kiss the ocean—tiny ripples forming, dissolving, vanishing into something vaster than themselves. They fall as strangers, yet in their descent, they find home.

I think of us, how we wandered into each other's orbit, separate yet drawn by unseen currents. We met like the rain meets the ocean—hesitant at first, uncertain in our falling. But love, like water, has a way of absorbing sorrow, carrying weight without breaking.

Perhaps that is what love is—an acceptance of dissolution, a surrender to something greater. We lose ourselves, not in erasure, but in becoming. In the vast, endless tide of each other, we remain, shifting, flowing, infinite.

37

Whispers of the Soul

There are moments in life when everything quiets down, and all that remains is the soft rhythm of your own heartbeat. In those spaces, time becomes an illusion. It's like standing at the edge of a memory, watching it unfold in a gentle haze of golden light. The past lingers, not as a shadow, but as a presence—comforting, familiar, and achingly close.

You can almost hear the words unsaid, the laughter that once filled the air, and the silences that spoke volumes. It's as if the world slows down to let you hold onto those fragments of love, of connection, of moments shared. They don't vanish; they settle into the corners of your heart, like letters imploding within, waiting to be read by the soul when it needs to feel close again.

In these quiet moments, you realize that the things we often search for—affirmation, purpose, direction—are already within us. They've always been there, nestled between the quiet hum of daily life and the rush of the world. All it takes is a moment of stillness to hear them, to feel them, to remember who we are when the noise fades away.

And so, we learn that the most intimate moments aren't the ones filled with grand gestures or loud declarations—they're the ones when everything else falls away, and we simply exist, breathing in the spaces where love once lived, where it still quietly thrives.

38

Ephemeral Grace

Beauty's absolution lies in the embrace of nothingness, in the quiet surrender of form to the infinite. It is not in the grandeur of what is seen but in the spaces left untouched—the pause between notes, the silence after laughter, the breath held before confession. It is the petal that falls before it is plucked, the wave that retreats before it crashes, the touch that lingers in the absence of hands.

We search for beauty in permanence, in the things we can hold, but it was never meant to be captured. It dissolves the moment we claim it, slipping through grasping fingers like dust kissed by the wind. Perhaps that is its mercy, its absolution—to belong to nothing, to no one. To exist only in the fleeting, the almost, the vanishing.

And so we stand, witnesses to the impossible, watching as beauty unfolds and unravels all at once. Not to own it, not to understand it, but simply to be in its presence, for a moment, before it fades into the quiet embrace of nothingness once more.

39

When Your Eyes Saw Me

Your gaze found me in the hush of an unguarded moment, and I felt the weight of being known. It was not the kind of seeing that skims the surface, but the kind that reaches into the marrow, the kind that names what I had left unnamed. And so, I withdrew—not out of fear, but because I was not ready for the truth your eyes held.

I became the shadow slipping behind a door, the breath swallowed before it could tremble. I turned into the silence between heartbeats, the space between footsteps. You called my name without speaking, and I answered in absence.

Perhaps it was never about hiding, but about finding myself in the vanishing. Perhaps some souls are meant to exist in the periphery—close enough to be felt, but never quite held. And perhaps, when your eyes saw me, I did not disappear. I only became what I was always meant to be—an echo lingering just beyond reach.

40

Past & Present

Touching you is as close as touching myself—a collision of past and present, of what was and what will be. In the press of skin, I recognize something long forgotten, a memory rising from the quiet depths, pulling me back into the shape I once abandoned.

You are not a stranger; you are the echo of a past life, the whisper of a thousand selves I have been and lost. In your presence, I see the reflection of my own becoming—the unraveling, the rebuilding, the endless cycle of return.

To reach for you is to reach for the self I have yet to meet. And in that moment, I am born again—not as something new, but as something remembered.

41

Weeping Mirror

When you cry, it is my tears that you shed—grief spilling from the places where our edges blur, where the line between you and I ceases to exist. Your sorrow pools in my palms, your tremble runs through my bones, and I wonder if pain has ever truly belonged to just one heart.

We are stitched together by something unseen, something older than names, older than time. When your voice breaks, it is my silence that answers. When you falter, it is my breath that steadies. I do not know where you end and I begin—perhaps we were never meant to be separate.

So cry, love, and I will feel it for you. Break, and I will carry the pieces. If I must weep so that you may breathe, then let me drown so that you may rise.

42

Ocean of Your Eyes

Your eyes—vast, fathomless—pull me under with a quiet gravity. They are the ocean without shore, the tide that knows no retreat. I fall into their depths, not drowning, but dissolving, my edges blurred by the current of something deeper than longing, older than time.

What secrets rest in their abyss? What forgotten storms have passed beneath their surface? I do not ask, for some mysteries are not meant to be answered—only felt, only surrendered to.

So I let myself sink, let the waves claim me. If I am to be lost, let it be here, in the endless fathoms of you, in the bottomless ocean of your eyes. Your eyes are where I stop breathing.

43

End of Longing

You are not the echo of my desire, not the ghost of longing that lingers in empty corridors. You are the hush after the storm, the final note that dissolves into silence.

I searched for you in echoes, in the endless reverberations of want, but you did not arrive as an answer—I found you as a closing, a full stop where I had only known ellipses. You did not stir the ache within me; you stilled it. You did not feed the hunger; you ended it.

Perhaps this is what desire was always meant to become—not an endless reaching, but a quiet arrival. Not a fire, but the gentle dark that follows when it has burned itself out.

44

Absence of Fear

I fear that I do not fear—that the hollow where terror once lived has become too quiet, too still. Once, my pulse raced at the thought of losing, of falling, of breaking. Now, the cliff's edge is just another place to stand, the abyss below just another shade of dark.

Is this freedom or surrender? A release or a reckoning? To feel nothing where fear should be—is it strength, or have I simply become nothing itself?

Perhaps fear was the tether that kept me from vanishing. Perhaps, in losing it, I have unmoored myself from the gravity of being. Perhaps, in this weightless drifting, I am already gone.

45

Withering

The day you left, the bougainvillea withered—petals curling inward, retreating into themselves as if they, too, felt the absence settle in the air. The vines, once wild with colour, now hung limp against the wall, their brightness leached by the hush you left behind.

I traced the brittle edges between my fingers, wondering if love, too, crumbles when left untended. If absence is a drought, if distance is a slow decay. The wind carried away the last of the petals, and I did not try to catch them. Every petal knows its way to find home.

But even as they faded, I knew—come another season, the bougainvillea would bloom again.

46

Hreem

There are moments when you implode—like stardust evaporating into the vacuum, unseen, unheard, yet infinitely expansive. These moments announce themselves with a force both overwhelming and tender—like the sky just before it tears open, carrying with it both sorrow and beauty. The rain pours, but each drop, though heavy, falls with such deliberate grace that it is impossible to mourn the storm.

When she arrives, you notice her feet first—her sandals a soft tap on the earth, like the rhythm of a forgotten song. Then comes the wave of her saree, the delicate fragrance of musk roses trailing in the air, a scent so familiar it stirs something deep within. Her neck tilts, two crescent moons carved in the space between her shoulders and chin—the same shape that adorns the head of the one you revere.

She smiles, but the smile never quite reaches her eyes, and in that fraction of an instant, you feel your heart crack, not with the violence of a break, but with the slow, inevitable surrender of a riverbank yielding to a torrential storm. Still, she leads you to the voices around you, voices that you strain to hear, yet they dissolve into the vast silence—because your every thought is lost, swallowed whole, in the ocean of her eyes.

She smiles at your words, but her gaze slips away, out the window, toward the endless horizon, to nothing you can touch. It is then, in the space between the worlds, that her smile finally finds its home in her eyes, like a flickering lamp igniting before a sacred prayer. Her voice swells into music, an ancient melody that you know by heart, though you've never heard it before.

And then, like a fleeting whisper, she is gone, retreating into the dark depths of your mind, leaving behind only echoes—the warmth of her lamp, the reverence of her song, and the quiet hum of her prayer. The waves of her ocean stutter and falter, leaving you adrift in the vast, still silence between the breaths she left behind.

47

The Practice of Joy

Consciousness is a practice—an art of finding exuberance in the quietest of moments, a ritual of welcoming joy as it arrives, again and again, like waves breaking on the shore. Each thought, a spark of something new, ignites with the brilliance of a thousand epiphanies—each one, like a bloom unfolding, only to fold back again into the soil of understanding.

We move through the world as though it is a dance, a series of movements that repeat, yet never the same. In each repetition, we find something deeper, something that was hidden in plain sight. The act of seeing, of being awake, becomes an offering—a grace we extend to ourselves and to the world, a reminder that life, in all its imperfection, is a continuous gift.

Joy does not come as a singular burst; it comes in quiet whispers, in the forgotten corners of a long day, in the slow unraveling of truths we have known all along. Consciousness is not an end, but a series of beginnings—a practice of embracing what rises within us, of surrendering to the constant unfolding of who we are.

48

Fireflies of a New Dawn

Fireflies made of golden sand, each one a fleeting spark, a confetti of transient lights flickering in the vast tapestry of epiphanies—these are the moments when time pauses, holding its breath, waiting for the next revelation. There is a certain sunshine on midnight, casting its glow where darkness dares to stretch, illuminating the quiet places that have never known such warmth. The sun wears its heart on its sleeves, unashamed of its vulnerability, offering light even to the shadows that would rather remain unseen.

A serpent coils around a finger with attentive grace, as if listening to a language only it understands—delicate and deliberate in its movement, as if time itself bends to its will. Somewhere, a word loops in a circle, spiraling through a different universe, its meaning slipping between the cracks of reality, just out of reach but always present.

And then, a smile—deliberately arced in wanton abandon—becomes the space where all these things meet. It is not a smile of restraint or reason, but one born of freedom, unchained from expectation. It is the unspoken connection between all things, the quiet understanding that everything is, and always has been, a beautiful, chaotic dance.

49

Keepers of Your Fire

Seek those who fan your flames—the ones who do not shrink from the heat of your being, but stand beside you, offering breath, stoking the embers until they burn brighter, wilder. They are the ones who see your spark and do not fear it, who understand that a flame is not just to be guarded, but to be nurtured, to be fed with the air of possibility and the fuel of belief.

They are not the ones who pull away when your fire becomes too much, too intense; instead, they lean in closer, reveling in the glow of your truth. In their presence, you do not need to hide your light or dim it to make others comfortable. With them, your flames become a language all their own, one that speaks not in words, but in warmth, in connection, in a quiet understanding that together, you burn brighter than you ever could alone.

Seek them out—those who are not afraid of your fire, who only wish to see it grow, who find joy in the heat of your spirit. For in their company, you will learn the true power of your flame—not as something to keep to yourself, but as something to share, to give, to transform the world around you.

50

Metamorphosis

This heart has weathered—shaped by all it has consumed, worn by the intensity of its storms and the heat of its fires. I am a creature of constant metamorphosis, unraveling with every breath we share, reshaping myself in response to every glance, every touch, every word. It is a transformation I cannot resist, for your love moves through me like a river—carving new paths, smoothing rough edges, yet never leaving me as I was before.

With every layer I shed, I am both broken and remade, caught between destruction and rebirth. The version of me that existed before is now a memory, leaving only fragments of who I once was. And yet, even in this disintegration, I find something more—something richer, deeper, more aligned with who I am meant to be.

Your love has weathered me, yes. But in this weathering, I have found that the end is not an ending at all. It is only the beginning—the start of something more, something eternal, something that stretches beyond the destruction into the endless possibility of who I can become.